The HAUNTED LIBRARY

IN LOVING MEMORY OF
THE REAL WBOLBB

I WISH YOU COULD'VE READ THIS ONE, DAD—DHB

* * * * * * * * * * * * * * * * *

I'd like to thank Mike Gruber (WIMG) for patiently answering questions while I wrote this book. I'd also like to thank Pieta Pemberton for sometimes knowing my series world better than I know it myself, and everyone at Grosset & Dunlap for their hard work on my behalf.

* * * * * * * * * * * * * * * * *

GROSSET & DUNLAP
Published by the Penguin Group
Penguin Group (USA) LLC, 375 Hudson Street, New York, New York 10014, USA

USA | Canada | UK | Ireland | Australia | New Zealand | India | South Africa | China
penguin.com
A Penguin Random House Company

Library of Congress Control Number: 2014039985

ISBN 978-0-448-46248-6 (pbk)   10 9 8 7 6 5 4 3
ISBN 978-0-448-46249-3 (hc)   10 9 8 7 6 5 4 3 2 1

The HAUNTED LIBRARY

THE FIVE O'CLOCK GHOST

BY DORI HILLESTAD BUTLER

ILLUSTRATED BY AURORE DAMANT

GROSSET & DUNLAP * AN IMPRINT OF PENGUIN GROUP (USA) LLC

GHOSTLY GLOSSARY

EXPAND
When ghosts make themselves larger

GLOW
What ghosts do so humans can see them

HAUNT
Where ghosts live

PASS THROUGH
When ghosts travel through walls, doors, and other solid objects

SHRINK
When ghosts make themselves smaller

SKIZZY
When ghosts feel sick to their stomachs

SOLIDS
What ghosts call humans, animals, and objects they can't see through

SPEW
What comes out when ghosts throw up

SWIM
When ghosts move freely through the air

WAIL
What ghosts do so humans can hear them

CHAPTER 1

A NEW CASE

W oof! Woof!"

"Cosmo! No!" Kaz grabbed Cosmo about a second and a half before he passed through the craft-room window and into the Outside. Kaz peered out the window. He didn't see what his dog was all excited about.

"You can't go into the Outside," Kaz scolded. "What are you thinking?"

Cosmo lowered his eyes. His tail drooped.

"He's a dog, Kaz," Claire said, glancing up from her homework. "He doesn't know it's dangerous for ghosts to be outside." Claire reached out to pet Cosmo. But Claire was a solid, so her hand passed through him.

"He *should* know," Kaz said, holding his dog tight against his chest. "He's seen what happens when ghosts go into the Outside."

Kaz and Cosmo used to live in an old schoolhouse with Kaz's mom and dad; his grandmom and grandpop; his little brother, Little John; and his big brother, Finn. Finn liked to stick his arm or leg through the wall to the Outside just to scare Kaz and Little John. But one day when the ghost boys were playing Keep Away, Finn stuck his head a little too far through the wall, and his whole

body was *pullllled* into the Outside. Grandmom and Grandpop tried to rescue Finn, but they ended up in the Outside, too. And they all blew away.

"Plus, Cosmo has been in the Outside himself, too," Kaz reminded Claire.

Last summer some solids came to the old schoolhouse with their big trucks and their wrecking ball. They destroyed the old schoolhouse, and the rest of Kaz's family was forced into the Outside. Like Finn, Grandmom, and Grandpop, they were all scattered in the wind. Kaz ended up here at the library. He felt lucky to have found Cosmo a few weeks ago when he and Claire were out solving a ghostly mystery. He hadn't seen anyone else in his family for so long.

Now Cosmo wiggled and squirmed

in Kaz's arms. Kaz hugged him even harder.

"I don't think your dog likes to be held so tight, Kaz," Beckett said. Beckett was the other ghost who lived at the library. He'd been here way longer than Kaz had.

Kaz loosened his grip on Cosmo, and the ghost dog pawed his way out of Kaz's arms. He paddled right back toward the window.

Kaz sighed. *What is* out *there?* he wondered. Cosmo had never been so interested in the Outside before.

"Claire, could you please close that shade?" Kaz asked, grabbing his dog again. "If Cosmo can't see what's out there, then maybe he'll settle down."

"Why don't *you* close the shade, Kaz?" Beckett said.

"I can't," Kaz said. And Beckett knew he couldn't.

Kaz simply didn't have the skills that other ghosts did. He was working on them. Really, he was. But ghost skills were hard. And he didn't like to practice. What ghost did?

"How do you know you can't close that shade?" Beckett asked. "Have you tried?"

"That's right, Kaz," Claire said. "Now that you can pick up solid objects, maybe you *can* pull the shade."

Kaz had only just learned to pick up solid objects. He still wasn't very good at it. And picking up a solid object wasn't the same as pulling on a shade and making it move.

But he was willing to give it a try.

With one arm wrapped firmly around

Cosmo, Kaz grabbed the shade with his other hand and *pulllllled* it down.

The shade didn't move.

"Squeeze it harder," Claire suggested.

Kaz squeezed harder, but his thumb passed through the shade.

Claire went over and yanked on the shade. Cosmo let out a low groan as it came down over the window.

"Now you can be free," Kaz said as he opened his arms and released his dog.

Beckett clucked his tongue. "How will Kaz learn to do things for himself if you do everything for him?" he asked Claire.

Before Claire could answer, her phone rang. She grabbed it from the table. "Hello? . . . Yes . . . Yes, it's true; I'm a ghost detective . . ." She tucked a strand of hair behind her ear and grinned at Kaz. "It means I solve ghostly mysteries . . .

Yes . . . Yes . . . of course! What is your address? . . . Okay, I'll be right there. Wait, how did you hear about me? . . . Cool! Yeah, okay. I'll be right there."

Claire stuffed her phone inside her front pants pocket. "Guess what, Kaz? We have a new case!" She closed her schoolbooks and stacked them in the middle of the table. "Do you remember Jonathan from the school play?"

"Of course," Kaz said. He and Claire had just solved the case of the ghost backstage a couple of weeks ago. Jonathan wasn't just involved in the case; he saw Kaz's mom at Claire's school! But by the time Kaz got there, his mom was long gone. She left behind a bead from her necklace, though. Kaz still carried it in his front pocket.

"Well, Jonathan has a friend named

David," Claire explained. "David Jeffrey, I think he said his name was. Anyway, David has a ghost in his house."

"What kind of ghost?" Kaz asked as he squeezed the ghost bead in his pocket. *Is it someone from my family? Is it my mom?*

"I don't know," Claire said. "David hasn't actually seen the ghost, so he can't describe it. But it turns on lamps, it makes the garage door go up, and it messes up their TV. I told him I'd come take a look."

"You're not going to go now, are you?" Beckett asked.

"Yes, we are," Claire said as she reached for her water bottle. Kaz always traveled with Claire inside her water bottle.

"But your homework isn't done," Beckett objected. "Kaz hasn't practiced his ghost skills. And it's almost time for dinner!"

Ghosts like Kaz and Beckett never ate dinner or any other meals. But Claire ate dinner every single day. Usually with her family.

"So?" Claire twisted the top off her water bottle. "You're not in charge of me, Beckett. And you're not in charge of Kaz, either. You're not our dad."

Claire was right. Beckett wasn't Kaz's pops. But he was the closest thing Kaz had to a parent here at the library.

"I don't know," Kaz said as Cosmo swam toward the window again.

Cosmo nudged the solid shade aside with his nose, but Kaz quickly scooped him up. "Maybe we should wait until tomorrow to go," Kaz said to Claire. He wasn't sure about leaving Cosmo right now.

Claire shook her head. "We have to go now," she said. "This ghost is different from other ghosts. It only comes out at five o'clock."

CHAPTER 2

THE FIVE O'CLOCK GHOST

Kaz wanted to go with Claire. He wanted to see whether the five o'clock ghost was someone from his family. But what if Cosmo passed through that window while Kaz was out with Claire? What if Cosmo blew away?

"I better not," Kaz said, holding tight to his dog. "I should stay here and keep an eye on Cosmo."

"Cosmo can shrink," Claire pointed

out. "We could bring him in the water bottle with us."

Hmm, Kaz thought. *We could . . .*

"He might get even *more* riled up if you take him with you," Beckett warned. "Whatever's got him so excited is in the Outside."

Okay, maybe not, Kaz thought.

"Yes, but Kaz will hold on to Cosmo," Claire told Beckett. "Come on, Kaz. You have to come with me. We're C *and* K Ghost Detectives. We solve cases together." She held the open water bottle out to him.

Beckett shrugged. "It's up to you, Kaz," he said. "As Claire pointed out, I'm not in charge of you."

Kaz didn't know what to do. On the one hand, it was nice to make decisions for himself. On the other hand, sometimes making decisions was hard.

"Okay," he said finally. "I'll come."

"Yay!" said Claire as Beckett shook his head in disapproval.

Kaz let Cosmo go again. Then he shrank down . . . down . . . down and swam inside Claire's water bottle.

"Woof! Woof!" Cosmo barked at Kaz.

The dog looked HUGE to Kaz from inside the water bottle.

"Come here, boy!" Kaz clapped his hands together. "You've ridden in Claire's bottle before. All you have to do is shrink!"

Cosmo sniffed the bottle. He let out another short bark, then shrank down . . . down . . . down and swam inside the bottle with Kaz.

"Good job," Claire said as she plopped the top on. "Let's go!" She hurried toward the entryway, the water bottle swinging at her side. Beckett drifted after them.

"Grandma?" Claire called.

"In here," Grandma Karen called back from the fiction room.

Claire poked her head around the corner. "I need to go out for a little bit. Is that okay?"

Grandma Karen glanced up at the clock on the wall behind her desk. "Now?" she asked. "It's almost dinnertime."

"Isn't that what I said?" Beckett asked Claire and Kaz.

Grandma Karen could see and hear ghosts when she was Claire's age, but she couldn't do it anymore. She knew that Claire saw ghosts, though. And she knew that Kaz, Beckett, and Cosmo lived here in the library. She even knew that Claire and Kaz were trying to find Kaz's family. Claire's parents didn't know any of that.

"It's *important*," Claire said, patting her water bottle. She had to be careful what she said, because there were other solids in the fiction room. Solids who didn't know about Kaz or Beckett or Cosmo.

Grandma Karen understood what Claire was trying to say. "Well, your

parents *are* away at that convention this week. I guess you and I can have dinner a little later tonight," she said.

"What about her homework?" Beckett cried, throwing his hands up in the air. "Aren't you going to ask her about her homework?"

"I want you home before dark," Grandma Karen said to Claire.

"Okay." Claire nodded. "Thanks, Grandma."

Beckett groaned. "You are entirely too easy on that child when her parents are away," he told Grandma Karen.

Once Kaz and Claire were outside, Claire took out her phone to get directions to David's house. "It's not far," she said as she marched up the street.

Cosmo's ears stood straight up and his nose twitched. Something in the

Outside had caught his attention again. Kaz tightened his hold on his dog.

Claire turned a corner, and they saw a solid dog and its owner coming toward them. The dog was on a leash, jogging beside a woman who had buds in her ears.

"Woof! Woof!" Cosmo barked at the jogger and her dog.

"WOOF! WOOF!" the solid dog barked back as it lunged at Claire's water bottle. That dog was smaller than Cosmo when Cosmo was his normal size, but it had a much scarier bark.

"Daisy! No!" The woman jerked on the leash and pulled her dog back. She walked way around Claire on the grass.

Cosmo struggled to break free from Kaz, but Kaz held on tight.

The woman pulled one of the buds

from her ears. "I'm sorry," she said to Claire as her dog continued to bark at Cosmo. "Daisy doesn't usually bark or jump on people like that."

"It's okay," Claire said, hurrying past the woman.

"Cosmo and I shouldn't have come," Kaz moaned.

"Why?" Claire asked, hoisting her water bottle back onto her shoulder. "He won't go anywhere as long as you're holding on to him. You worry too much, Kaz."

Kaz couldn't help worrying. Cosmo was the only family Kaz had right now.

"I don't think it's much farther," Claire said, checking the map on her phone. "We're on the right street."

They walked a little farther, and Kaz heard violin music. It came from a small

black box on the grass. *A radio,* Kaz thought. Claire's grandma had one in the library.

A woman around Grandma Karen's age was sitting on a little stool beside the radio and planting some flowers. She looked up at Claire. "Hello," she said.

"Hi," Claire said, stopping on the sidewalk. "I'm looking for the Jeffreys' house. Do you know them?"

"Yes, they live right over there." The woman pointed to a yellow house down the street.

"Thanks," Claire said. The water bottle banged against her hip as she skipped over to the yellow house.

A boy who was a little shorter than Claire opened the door before Claire even knocked. "Are you Claire?" he asked.

"Yes. You must be David," Claire replied.

The boy nodded as he held the screen door for Claire. "Come on in. The ghost will be here soon." He had a serious look on his face.

Claire twisted the top off her water bottle, and Kaz and Cosmo swam out. They both expanded to their usual size and wafted around the room. It was the sort of room Claire called a "living room." It had a couch and two chairs, a TV, and some sort of musical instrument sitting in the corner. A cartoon show played on the TV. The volume was turned down low. The only light in the room came from the TV.

Kaz didn't see any ghosts.

"So . . . do you want me to look around for your ghost?" Claire asked David.

"No," David said. He shivered as Kaz floated past him. "Just wait. It'll come out at five o'clock sharp."

But Kaz couldn't wait. Not if there was a chance this ghost was someone

from his family. "Hello?" he called. "Mom? Pops? Grandmom? Grandpop? Little John? Finn? Are any of you here?"

No response.

Holding tight to Cosmo, Kaz swam through a kitchen . . . a bathroom . . . and a messy kids' bedroom. He didn't see any ghosts in any of those rooms.

No ghosts in the grown-up's bedroom, either. It looked like just a mom lived here. There weren't any dad clothes in the closet.

Kaz made his way into a third bedroom. A solid teenage girl sat cross-legged on her bed, her eyes fixed on the cell phone in her hand.

Kaz hovered over the girl's shoulder to see what she found so interesting. He watched as the girl typed with her thumbs:

The clock on the girl's phone read 4:55 p.m. Kaz didn't want to miss whatever was going to happen at five o'clock, so he swam back to the living room. Claire and David stared at the clock above the TV.

Claire turned to raise an eyebrow at

Kaz. Since she couldn't talk to Kaz in front of David, that was her way of asking him whether he saw anything interesting.

Kaz shook his head.

They all watched the minutes tick by. 4:57 . . . 4:58 . . . 4:59 . . .

At exactly five o'clock, three things happened all at once:

(1) There was a loud, rumbly sound in another part of the house.

(2) A table lamp in the living room came on all by itself.

(3) The picture on the TV flickered, and a loud, SCARY man's voice boomed through the TV. "BLAH . . . BLAH . . . BLAH-BLAH . . . BLAH . . . BLAH . . . BLAH . . ."

"There's our ghost!" David announced. "Right on time."

CHAPTER 3

SEARCHING FOR GHOSTS

BLAH . . . BLAH . . . BLAH-BLAH . . . BLAH . . . BLAH . . . BLAH . . . BLUH-BLAH . . . BLUH-BLUH-BLUH . . . BLAH . . . BLAH-BLAH . . . BLAH . . . BLAH . . . BLAH . . ."

Wide lines ran across the TV screen in rhythm with the garbled voice.

While Claire and David stared at the TV, Kaz swam over to the lamp. He searched behind it and under the table it sat on. That lamp couldn't have come

on all by itself. A ghost with better ghost skills than Kaz probably turned it on and then swam into the TV.

"BLUH-BLUH-BLUH . . . BLAH . . . BLAH-BLUH . . ."

Claire squinted at the TV. "I can't understand what he's saying."

"Neither can I," David said.

Neither could Kaz. But the voice sounded angry. Very angry.

"Sometimes I can make out a word here or there," David said. "But most of the time I have no idea what he's yelling about."

Kaz swam over to the TV. "Hello?" he said to whoever might be hiding inside.

"BLAH . . . BLAH . . . BLAH-BLAH . . . BLAH . . . BLAH . . . BLAH . . . BLAH . . . BLAH . . . BLAH-BLAH . . . BLAH . . .

BLAH . . . BLAH . . . BLAH . . . BLAH . . .
BLAH-BLAH . . . BLAH . . . BLAH . . .
BLAH . . ."

Cosmo tilted his head at the TV. Before Kaz could stop him, the ghost dog scampered through the TV screen and disappeared.

Claire gasped.

"NO!" Kaz cried. He swam back and forth in front of the TV, not knowing what else to do. "Cosmo, come back! Hello? Who's in there? Whoever you are, is my dog in there with you?"

Or—Kaz gulped. Did Cosmo pass all the way through the TV *and* through the wall into the Outside?

Kaz sidestroked over to the window and looked out. He didn't see Cosmo anywhere in the Outside.

The voice stopped. The lines on the

TV disappeared, and the cartoon show returned.

"Is that it? Is the ghost done?" Claire asked.

Kaz stared at the TV. Cosmo hadn't returned.

"No," David said. "It'll start up again pretty soon."

As David predicted, the lines reappeared, and the angry, garbled voice returned a few seconds later. "BLAH . . . BLAH . . . BLAH-BLAH . . . BLAH . . . BLAH . . . BLAH . . ."

Kaz wanted to go inside that TV. He wanted to get Cosmo. And he wanted to see who was hiding in there. He was pretty sure it wasn't anyone from his family. His family would've come out when they heard Kaz's voice or when they saw Cosmo. But passing through

solid objects made Kaz feel skizzy. In fact, it made him feel *so* skizzy that he'd only done it once before in his entire life.

All of a sudden, Cosmo swam back through the TV. "Woof! Woof!" he barked as he sailed over to Kaz.

Kaz breathed a sigh of relief and grabbed his dog. "Cosmo! You're okay!" He hugged Cosmo. "So, what did you see in there? Who's inside that TV?"

Cosmo just licked Kaz's face. He couldn't answer Kaz's questions. Or if he could, Kaz wouldn't understand.

Claire pulled out her detective's book and jotted down some notes. Still holding tight to his dog, Kaz read over her shoulder.

Ghost Report:
David Jeffrey's house. 5:00 p.m.
The garage door went up.

A lamp came on.

Someone (a ghost?) started yelling through the TV, but we couldn't understand them.

The garage door must've made the rumbly sound Kaz heard when everything else started happening.

Thump, thump, thump came the sound of footsteps. It sounded like they were tramping up some stairs.

Another ghost?

The footsteps grew closer . . . and closer . . .

A small voice called from around the corner. *"Daaavid?"*

Everyone turned to the little boy who was standing in the doorway to the living room. He couldn't have been more than five or six years old. "Is Mom home?" the boy asked shyly as he hugged a toy car to his chest. A thin wire dangled from the top of the car.

"No, Ben," David replied. Apparently, Ben was David's little brother.

"But I heard the garage door go up," Ben said.

"I know," David said. "That happened yesterday, too, remember?"

"Why?" Ben asked. "Why does the garage door go up all by itself?"

"I don't know!" David said impatiently as he and Claire watched the lines on the TV.

"BLUH-BLUH-BLUH . . . BLAH . . . BLAH-BLAH . . . BLAH . . . BLAH . . ."

"And why is that scary man on all our TVs?" Ben asked.

"*All* your TVs?" Claire turned to the boy. "Is there someone talking on other TVs in your house?"

Ben nodded. "It's on the TV downstairs."

How could that be? Kaz wondered. A ghost couldn't be in a garage, inside this TV, and inside another TV all at once.

Unless there's more than one ghost.

"Claire!" Kaz exclaimed. "I think there's more than one ghost here. Maybe it's even a whole family of ghosts. We need to find that other TV!"

Claire nodded slightly as she wrote some more in her notebook. "Can we see this other TV?" she asked David and Ben. "You may have more than one ghost in your house."

"Ghost?" Ben's eyes went wide.

David led Claire around a corner and into the kitchen. He opened a door at the far end of the room, and he, Claire, and Ben clomped down some stairs. Kaz and Cosmo swam just above Ben's head.

The room at the bottom of the stairs was huge. And brightly lit. Kaz saw couches, chairs, and lots of toys scattered around. He also saw a TV. Like Ben said, there were lines and a strange voice on this TV, too: "BLAH . . . BLAH . . . BLAH-BLAH . . . BLAH . . . BLAH . . . BLAH . . . BLUH-BLAH . . . BLUH-BLUH-BLUH . . .

BLAH . . . BLAH-BLAH . . . BLAH . . . BLAH . . . BLAH . . ."

Kaz and Cosmo swam over. "Hello?" Kaz said into the TV. "Who's in there? Why are you haunting this house? You can tell me. I'm a ghost, too."

The garbled voice and the lines on the TV stopped. This time for good.

"So, what do you think?" David asked Claire.

"I don't know," Claire said, turning a page in her notebook. "Does this stuff

happen at five o'clock in the morning, too? Or just five o'clock in the afternoon?"

David thought for a second. "I don't know," he said. "Probably just five o'clock in the afternoon."

Claire wrote that down.

David folded his arms and tilted his head at Claire. "Are you really a ghost detective?" he asked. "Can you really find ghosts and get rid of them?"

"You're a ghost *detective*?" Ben cried.

"Yes." Claire shrugged as if it were no big deal. "And yes, of course, I can find them and get rid of them."

"How?" David asked. "You don't have anything to catch them with like the ghost hunters on TV do."

"I do at home!" Claire said.

"You do?" David, Ben, and Kaz said all at the same time.

This was news to Kaz.

"Yeah," Claire said uneasily. "I, uh, just don't usually bring it the first time I visit a client."

Kaz had never seen Claire use any equipment.

"Let me go over the notes I took today," Claire said, tucking her notebook inside her bag. "Then I'll come back again tomorrow. *With* my ghost-hunting equipment. I'll find your ghost, David. I promise!"

CHAPTER 4

CLAIRE'S EQUIPMENT

What ghost-hunting equipment?" Kaz asked, once he and Cosmo were safely inside Claire's water bottle and on their way back to the library. "What equipment do you have? And how are you going to use it to find David's ghost?"

"The thing is," Claire said as she looked both ways, then crossed a street, "I don't think David thinks I can solve this case."

Kaz wasn't so sure they could solve

this case, either. Not if the ghosts didn't want to come out from hiding.

"And he's right about equipment," Claire went on. "All the ghost hunters on TV have stuff to help them find ghosts. Remember, Mrs. Beesley asked about that, too, when she hired us to find the ghost in her attic. I don't need any equipment to find ghosts. But I might need it so people *think* I can find ghosts."

"What kind of equipment?" Kaz asked.

Claire shrugged. "I don't know yet."

Kaz hoped that whatever she came up with didn't scare the ghosts at David's house and make them even less likely to come out of hiding.

* * * * * * * * * * * * * * *

Later that night, after Claire and Grandma Karen had eaten dinner, Claire searched

the library basement for "ghost-hunting equipment."

She picked up a round glass object with a handle and held it to her left eye. It made her eye look really big.

"What is that?" Kaz wafted closer. He'd never seen such a thing before.

"A magnifying glass?" Beckett raised an eyebrow. "No one's going to believe a simple magnifying glass will help you find ghosts."

Claire scowled and put it back in the box.

"Why not?" Kaz asked. "It makes things bigger. So it should help you see things you wouldn't otherwise see."

"Things like ghosts?" Beckett snorted. He shook his head. "I don't think so."

Claire stepped over a box of old books and reached for another object. This thing covered both of her eyes.

"Binoculars?" Beckett asked.

"What are binoculars?" Kaz asked. He hovered in front of Claire. All he saw from this end was two dark circles.

"They're like magnifying glasses, only they help you see things that are far away," Claire explained. "People use them to watch birds and stuff."

"That's an even worse idea than the magnifying glass!" Beckett said.

"Yeah, you're probably right," Claire said as she returned the binoculars to the shelf.

Kaz scanned the boxes on the rest of the shelves while Beckett followed Claire to the other side of the basement.

"There's really no such thing as ghost-hunting equipment, you know," Beckett said. "A solid either sees ghosts or she doesn't—"

"Don't call us solids!" Claire said. Kaz knew Claire didn't like that word, so he tried not to use it around her. But Beckett seemed to use the word as often as he could.

"How about this?" Kaz reached for a— Actually, he had no idea what it was. He just hoped he could pick it up. *Concentrate . . . concentrate . . . concentrate . . . ,* he told

himself. He managed to raise the heavy, solid object a couple of inches above the box. But he could only hold on to it for a few seconds before it slipped through his hands and dropped back into the box.

Claire came over to see what Kaz had. "A mini vacuum?" she said as she picked it up and turned it all around. "Maybe. If it's charged."

"Really?" Beckett arched his eyebrows.

"Maybe," Claire said again, scanning the boxes on the shelves. She set the mini vacuum on the floor and reached for a box labeled ELECTRONICS. She pulled a long wire out of the box, then went back to get the magnifying glass. Finally she picked up the mini vacuum and tromped up two flights of stairs, carrying everything she had found.

Kaz and Beckett followed close behind.

Claire plugged the mini vacuum into the wall. "I can work on it while it's charging," she said as she went to the cabinet and pulled out a box that said ALUMINUM FOIL. She tore off long sheets of foil and wrapped them around the mini vacuum until the whole thing was covered.

Then she grabbed the long piece of wire and bent one end into a circle. "This is the antenna," she told Kaz as she wrapped the other end of the wire around the handle of the mini vacuum, twisting it to make it stay in place.

"Hmph," Beckett said.

"What's an antenna?" Kaz asked.

"Well, on a radio it's the thing that helps you find a station to listen to," Claire explained. "But on this, it's going to be the thing that helps me find ghosts."

Claire is so smart, Kaz thought.

"What do you think?" Claire asked, holding the foil-wrapped mini vacuum in one hand and the magnifying glass in the other. "I've got a special ghost glass to help me see ghosts. And a—what should I call this?" She thought for a second.

"A ghost detector? No, ghost *catcher* to help me find *and catch* ghosts."

"I think anyone who believes you're going to catch ghosts with that thing should have his head examined," Beckett said.

"Oh yeah?" Claire said. She unplugged the cord from the vacuum and pressed the button on top. The machine roared to life, making a horrible, HORRIBLE noise. Claire slowly raised her arm and aimed her "ghost catcher" at Beckett. It was obviously very strong, because it sucked the hat off his head and *pullllled* him toward the vacuum.

"Turn it off! Turn it off!" Beckett screamed as he flailed about.

Kaz put his hands over his eyes. He couldn't watch.

Claire turned the ghost catcher off.

"I don't know," she said with a smirk. "I'm pretty sure I could catch a ghost with this thing if I wanted to."

"Hmph!" Beckett said as he grabbed his hat, plopped it firmly on his head, then disappeared through the floor.

* * * * * * * * * * * * * *

"What is all that?" Grandma Karen asked Claire the next day.

It was four thirty—time to go back to

David's house. While Claire stuffed her new ghost-hunting equipment into her detective bag, Kaz tried to lure Cosmo away from the window. Again.

Cosmo and Claire's cat, Thor, had spent the entire day going from window to window and peering outside.

What in the world are they so interested in? Kaz wondered.

"It's stuff to find and catch ghosts," Claire said to Grandma Karen, holding

her bag open. "I can't tell people I can see ghosts. I need special equipment. Like the people on TV."

"I see," Grandma Karen said.

Claire bit her lip. "Do you think people will believe I can really find and catch ghosts with this stuff?" she asked.

Grandma Karen scratched her chin. "They will if their problems disappear after you leave. Are you going back to that boy's house again?"

Claire had to shift things in her bag to make it close. "Yes," she said. "Is that okay?"

"It's fine," Grandma Karen said. "You might want to take a look around when you step outside, though. A little boy just told me he saw a ghost boy out by our mailbox."

A ghost boy? Outside the library? That caught Kaz's attention.

Grandma Karen added, "I wouldn't have thought anything of it, except a little girl told me she saw a ghost over by the bushes yesterday. And I've noticed Thor has been spending a lot of time staring out the window."

So has Cosmo.

"Maybe there's a new ghost in the neighborhood," Grandma Karen said.

"We'll check it out," Claire said as she opened her water bottle.

Kaz grabbed Cosmo, and the two ghosts shrank down . . . down . . . down, then swam inside the bottle.

But when Claire took them into the Outside, none of them saw any ghosts.

They continued on to David's house. Along the way, they passed the same lady who had been planting flowers the day before. She was planting even more flowers today, and she had that same little radio on the ground next to her. But today there wasn't music coming out of it. There was talking: "You're listening to KQRC. Ninety-two point seven on your AM radio dial."

They arrived at David's house a few minutes before five o'clock. His living room looked the same as it did the day before. The TV was on. The lights were off.

Claire opened her water bottle, and Kaz and Cosmo swam out. Then she opened her overstuffed detective bag.

"Is that your equipment?" David asked.

"Yes," Claire said as she started taking things out.

David walked all around Claire. "Nice," he said. "So what does all this stuff do?" He reached for the foil-covered vacuum, but Claire yanked it away.

"It helps me detect ghosts. I can see them in here." She raised the magnifying glass. "This is my special ghost glass."

Kaz held his breath, wondering if David would believe Claire.

He seemed to. "Cool," David said, peering through the glass but not touching it. "Where did you get all this stuff? Did you order it online?"

"No, I built it myself," Claire said with a sideways glance at Kaz.

"Cool," David said again. "Well, it's almost five o'clock. We'll find out soon enough whether it actually works."

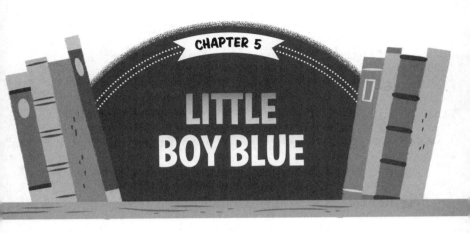

CHAPTER 5

LITTLE BOY BLUE

You came back," David's little brother, Ben, said as he strolled into the living room.

"Yes. I brought some special equipment this time to help me find your ghosts," Claire said. She peered at Ben through her "ghost glass." But neither Claire nor Kaz saw any ghosts.

Ben crossed his arms. "Ally says you're probably a fake," he told Claire.

"Who's Ally?" Claire asked.

"Our big sister," Ben replied.

"I didn't know you had a sister," Claire said to David.

David shrugged. "She's thirteen. She's supposed to watch us after school, but all she does is sit in her room and text her friends."

"I saw her yesterday," Kaz told Claire. "That's exactly what she was doing. Sitting in her room, texting her friends."

"Hm," Claire grunted. She shifted the antenna on her ghost catcher. Then with the ghost glass in one hand and the ghost catcher in the other, she started moving *sloooowly* around the room.

"Do you see any ghosts?" David asked. "Are they here yet?"

"I'm not sure," Claire said.

Ben set his car on the floor and wandered over to the musical instrument

in the corner. Kaz was curious what that instrument was, so he and Cosmo swam over to see. It had keys that looked like piano keys, but they weren't all on the same row. There were two rows. And lots of buttons.

Ben flipped a switch on the instrument, and the buttons labeled FLUTE 1, VIOLIN, and FRENCH HORN lit up. Ben started playing a song with one finger.

Kaz knew that song. It was called "Twinkle, Twinkle, Little Star." His mom used to sing it to him, Finn, and Little John.

"What are you doing, Ben?" David said. "You can't play the organ now."

"Why?" Ben asked.

"Because Claire's going to try to catch our ghosts, and we need to be able to hear them when they come," David explained.

"I don't want to hear them," Ben said.

He turned off the FLUTE 1 and VIOLIN buttons, and turned on the FLUTE 2 and CLARINET buttons. Then he started playing "Twinkle, Twinkle, Little Star" all over again. It sounded completely different with the different buttons pushed.

Kaz was fascinated. He noticed one of the buttons said TRIANGLE. Kaz loved the sound of a triangle. They'd had one back at the old schoolhouse. He wondered how "Twinkle, Twinkle, Little Star" would sound with the TRIANGLE button pushed.

Without thinking, Kaz touched his finger to the button. He'd never been able to turn a solid switch or push a solid button, so he didn't expect anything to happen. But the button slid forward . . . and when it did, the sound through the organ changed.

Kaz stared wide-eyed.

Ben pulled his fingers back from the keys as if he'd been burned. "D-did you see that?" he cried. "That button changed all by itself!"

"And it's not even five o'clock," David said. "The ghost is early today!"

Claire glared at Kaz, the ghost glass dangling at her side.

"Sorry," Kaz said to Claire, even though he didn't feel sorry. He, Kaz, had moved that button! All by himself. He hadn't even been trying to move it.

Kaz remembered the first time he ever picked up a solid object. It happened at Claire's school. He didn't think about it; he just went right over to that mean boy and grabbed the sword out of his hand.

Then there was the time he accidentally turned a solid lamp into a ghostly lamp. He'd actually been trying to flip the switch on the lamp, but somehow, without thinking about it, he had turned the whole lamp ghostly.

Was it possible Kaz sometimes tried *too hard* to master his ghost skills?

While Kaz was thinking about that,

the big hand on the clock inched toward the twelve. It was five o'clock. All at once, the garage door went up, the table lamp blinked on, and that same garbled voice that they'd all heard yesterday boomed into the room. But today that voice didn't come just through the TV. It also blared through the organ.

"Ahhh!" Ben cried, scooting the organ bench back.

Claire, Kaz, and David all backed up, too.

"Woof! Woof!" Cosmo barked at the organ.

The voice was loud and scary when it came through the TV. It was even louder and *scarier* when it came through the organ.

"Pick up that ghost glass!" David exclaimed. "Aim it over there." He pointed at the organ.

Claire turned her ghost glass toward the organ.

"I-I'm going to g-go get Ally," Ben said in a shaky voice. He ran down the hall.

"Do you see the ghost now?" David asked.

"Uh . . . ," Claire said. Neither Claire nor Kaz saw any ghost.

David scowled. "Does that thing really work?" he asked.

Kaz and Cosmo swam all around the organ. Was there a ghost hiding inside? There were tiny holes in the front of the organ where the sound came out. Kaz shrank down . . . down . . . down and tried to peer through those holes.

As he did, the voice BOOMED out again.

"Ahh!" Kaz shrieked, backing away. That voice was so LOUD.

But even though it was LOUD, Kaz, Claire, and David could understand the voice inside the organ a little better than they understood the voice inside the TV: "W . . . B . . . ZERO . . . BLAH . . . BLAH . . . BLAH."

Claire and David looked at each other. "W, B, Zero?" David asked. "What does that mean?"

Claire shrugged. She set her ghost glass down on the floor, pulled out her notebook, and started writing.

As she did, the voice continued: "BLAH . . . BLAH . . . BLAH . . . LITTLE BOY BLUE . . ."

Little Boy Blue?

"What's going on, David?" a teenage girl asked from the hallway. It was Ally, the same girl Kaz had seen texting on her phone yesterday. Ben sort of cowered behind her.

"Ben says there are ghosts in our living room and your friend is trying to catch them," Ally said.

"That's right," David said as Cosmo swam over to Ally.

"Well, where are they?" Ally looked right through Cosmo.

"Just wait," David said. "You won't see them, but you'll hear them. They're inside the TV and the organ. They'll start talking again." He scanned the room. "Any second now, they'll start talking."

They all waited.

And waited.

And waited some more.

But the ghostly voices seemed to have stopped.

"That's weird," David said, glancing up at the clock. "It usually goes on for, like, twenty minutes. I wonder why it stopped early today." He turned to Claire. "Did you catch the ghosts? Is that why everything stopped?"

"I don't think so," Claire said, shifting her ghost catcher.

Ally snorted. "Of course she didn't catch any ghosts. She's just a kid." She pulled her sweater tighter around her as Cosmo swam around her head and sniffed at her ponytail. "Are you guys *scared* to be here after school without Mom?"

"No!" David said at the same time Ben nodded his head hard.

"It's okay," Ally said soothingly. "When Mom gets home, you should tell her you're

scared to stay here alone. Tell her you want a grown-up babysitter."

"I don't want a grown-up babysitter," David said.

"I do!" Ben spoke up.

Kaz wafted over to the TV. "Hello?" he said, swimming back and forth in front of it. "Hello? Who's in there? We can't understand you when you talk to us from in there. We don't know what W-B-Zero is, and we don't know who Little Boy Blue is, and we can't understand anything else you're saying . . ."

Kaz waited for a ghost to talk back to him. When none did, he swam back to the organ.

"Hello? . . . Will *you* talk to me?" He peered through the tiny holes where the sound came through the organ, but he couldn't see anything inside. "Would you please come out so we can talk to you? . . . Who are you? . . . What do you want? . . . Why do you only talk to us at five o'clock?"

But the ghosts didn't come out. And they didn't answer any of Kaz's questions.

CHAPTER 6

THINKING THINGS OVER

"Mom!" Ally cried the second Mrs. Jeffrey walked in the door. "Mom, you've got to find somebody else to take care of the kids."

Cosmo's nose was practically glued to Ally's head. He sniffed and pawed at the little ball on top of her ponytail.

"Ally," Mrs. Jeffrey said as she sorted through the mail. "We've been over this. I know you'd like to see your friends after school—"

"No, it's not about that," Ally said. She swatted at Cosmo as though she could feel him messing with her ponytail, but her hand went right through him.

"Then what is it about?" Mrs. Jeffrey asked.

"David and Ben are *scared* to stay home alone without an adult. Right, guys?" Ally raised her eyebrows at them.

"Yes," Ben said at the same time David said, "Well—"

Mrs. Jeffrey turned to Ben with concern. "What are you scared of?" she asked.

"Ghosts," Ben said.

"There's no such thing as ghosts," Mrs. Jeffrey said.

Kaz groaned. He didn't like it when solid people said that.

"There is, too," Ben said. "They come

to our house every day at five o'clock!"

"Mom," Ally said, worming her way in between Ben and their mother. "Ava's mom watches little kids after school. She said she would *love* to have David and Ben."

"You know we can't afford a babysitter, Ally," Mrs. Jeffrey said. She set the mail on the counter.

"Ava's mom says you don't have to pay—"

Mrs. Jeffrey shook her head. "I can't let her do that. But both boys have dentist appointments on Monday. You can see your friends then. Other than that, I need you here after school. I'm sorry, honey."

"One day off. Big whoop," Ally grumbled as she left the room.

Cosmo started to follow Ally, but Kaz called, "Cosmo! Stay here!"

The ghost dog let out a low groan and swam back to Kaz.

"Good boy," Kaz said, giving his dog a pat.

Then Mrs. Jeffrey noticed Claire. "Who are you?" she asked, glancing curiously at the things in Claire's hands.

"This is Claire," David said. "She's here to help us get rid of our ghosts."

"I see," Mrs. Jeffrey said with a tight smile. Kaz had a feeling Mrs. Jeffrey didn't believe Claire could do that.

"It's nice to meet you, Claire," Mrs. Jeffrey said. "But I think it's time for you to go home."

"Okay," Claire said. She opened her water bottle, and Kaz and Cosmo quickly swam inside. Then she shoved everything else in her bag and headed for the door.

"Wait." Mrs. Jeffrey called her back. She handed her a magazine called *CQ*. It was addressed to someone named J. C. Hill. "This mail was delivered here by mistake. Would you mind dropping it off at the next-door neighbors' house on your way home?"

"Sure," Claire said, taking the magazine. "Bye, David. I'll see you tomorrow."

Claire glanced down at the address on the magazine, then up at the house numbers. "I think it's that house over there," she said, walking over. She put J. C. Hill's magazine in the mailbox, then adjusted the strap of her water bottle and started for home.

"Those are strange ghosts at that house," Kaz said. "They only come out at five o'clock. They do the same thing every day: They turn on a lamp, they open the garage door, and they mess up the TVs. But then they stay there inside the TVs and the organ. They don't come out and glow or wail or anything."

Claire nodded. "It makes me wonder if there's another explanation for what's happening at David's house."

"Like what?" Kaz asked.

"I don't know," Claire said.

Kaz and Claire walked in silence for a while, each lost in their own thoughts.

If ghosts aren't turning on the lamp, opening the garage door, and talking through the TVs and the organ, then solids *are doing those things,* Kaz thought. *But how could a solid person climb inside a TV or an organ? How could they do all those things without David or Ben or Ally or Claire or me seeing them?*

Also, *what does W-B-Zero mean? Who is Little Boy Blue? And why does everything always happen at five o'clock?*

"We know David's not the so-called ghost." Claire made quotation marks in the air. "He's the one who hired us. And I don't think Ben is the ghost. But what about Ally? Did you notice that the scary voice stopped when she came into the room?"

Kaz hadn't noticed. But now that he thought about it, he realized Claire was right.

"Everything always happens when she's out of the room," Kaz said. "Plus, she doesn't like taking care of her brothers after school. I saw her texting with her friends yesterday. She told one of her friends that she actually had a *plan* to get out of taking care of them."

"Well, that's interesting," Claire said. "Maybe her plan is to make her brothers so scared to stay home after school that their mom has to find another place for them to go. But how is she doing all these things?"

Kaz thought for a minute. "She's got one of those fancy phones like yours. Maybe she's doing it all with her phone."

Claire let out a small laugh. "You think there could be apps to make your garage door go up and to turn on lights and make voices come through TVs and organs?"

"Maybe," Kaz said. He didn't know all the things solids could do with their phones. But he'd sure seen Claire do a lot with hers.

Claire shrugged. "I suppose it's possible."

They were back at the library now. But instead of going inside, Claire pulled out her phone. "Huh," she said after a few seconds. "There *is* an app that lets you open your garage door and turn on lights from far away. And I know there are also lamps that come on if you clap your hands or make a loud noise. That voice is really loud. Maybe Ally hid some sort of recording device around the TV or the organ. You know, like my grandma did a few months ago." Claire scratched her head. "But what about those lines on the TV? How could she have done that?"

Kaz had no idea.

"And if she did put some sort of recording device near the TV or the organ, why is the recording so hard to understand?" Claire asked.

Kaz didn't know that, either.

"Is there anyone else who could be doing all this stuff?" he asked.

Claire shrugged. "A real ghost? Or several ghosts. Maybe they just don't want to come out for some reason."

"Maybe," Kaz said.

"Or maybe it's somebody we haven't met yet. Or somebody we've completely overlooked," Claire said.

* * * * * * * * * * * * * * *

That night, while Claire was asleep, Kaz heard a strange noise in the library entryway.

"What was that?" Kaz asked Beckett.

The ghosts were hanging out in the fiction room. Beckett was trying to turn a solid book into a ghostly book, but he wasn't having much luck.

"What was what?" Beckett asked, annoyed.

"You didn't hear that?" Kaz asked. He tilted his head toward the entryway to see if he would hear it again. "At first it sounded like a book being dropped in the book drop, but then I thought I heard . . . *wailing*."

"Ghost wailing?" Beckett said.

Kaz nodded.

Both ghosts floated as still as they possibly could. Kaz didn't even breathe. He just listened.

And a few minutes later, they both heard a low, ghostly "WOOOOOOOOOOOO!"

CHAPTER 7

ANOTHER GHOST

osmo led Kaz and Beckett to the library entryway. He swam over to the book drop and sniffed at it. "WOOF! WOOF!" he barked, his tail swishing from side to side. But it wasn't an angry bark; it was a happy bark.

"Cosmo?" came a small voice from inside the book drop.

Kaz's jaw fell open. *He knew that voice.* "Little John?"

"Kaz?" The face of a young ghost boy

appeared through the wall of the book drop.

"LITTLE JOHN!" Kaz rushed forward. "It *is* you!"

The rest of Little John passed through the book drop, and the two ghost brothers hugged and danced around. Cosmo was so excited, he could hardly contain himself. He leaped at Little John and licked him all over.

"Where did you come from? How did you get here? Are you staying?" Kaz had so many questions.

"Staying?" Beckett said. "You mean I'm going to have *two* kids and a dog to take care of?"

"You do *not* have to take care of us," Kaz told Beckett.

For just a second, Beckett looked hurt. Or disappointed. Or *something*. Was it

possible he actually *liked* taking care of
Kaz and Cosmo?

"Who's that?" Little John asked Kaz.

"His name is Beckett," Kaz said. "He
lives here, too. Beckett, this is my brother
Little John."

"I figured," Beckett said.

"How long have you been here?"
Little John asked Kaz.

"Since our haunt got torn down," Kaz replied. "The wind blew me in through a window. What happened to you when our haunt got torn down?"

"First, I got blown into a barn," Little John said, wrinkling his nose. "There were lots of solid cows in there. They kept mooing at me. And they smelled bad. I didn't like it there, so I left."

"You went into the Outside on purpose?" Kaz cried. Ghosts never went into the Outside on purpose.

"It was better than staying in that barn," Little John said as he scratched Cosmo's ears.

"What happened next?" Kaz asked.

"The wind blew me into a house. There was a ghost family and a solid family living there. One of the ghost girls was six years old, just like me," Little John said. "At night, we liked to glow and scare the solid kids!"

"Little John!" Kaz scolded.

"What? It was fun." Little John giggled. Then he turned serious. "Those ghosts told me I might find our family in the library. So I rode the wind here. But it kept blowing me *past* the library instead of *inside* the library."

"I wonder if Cosmo saw you," Kaz said. "Maybe that's why he's been acting so crazy lately!" Kaz had to admit, Cosmo looked pretty calm right now.

"How did you finally get in here?" Beckett asked Little John. "Seems to me it would be even harder to come in through the book drop than to pass through a wall."

"Not if you're inside a book!" Little John grinned. "When I couldn't get inside the library, I let the wind carry me to another house. The people there had library books, so I went inside one and waited for them to take the book back to the library!"

Kaz and Little John spent the rest of the night catching up while Cosmo dog-paddled around them. Eventually, Kaz told Little John about Claire and about C & K Ghost Detectives.

Little John gaped at Kaz. "You made friends with a *solid*?" he cried. "Do Mom and Pops know?"

"No. I haven't seen Mom and Pops since our haunt got torn down," Kaz said.

"You haven't?" Little John said. "You mean, Mom's not here?"

"No," Kaz replied. "What makes you think she'd be here?"

Little John reached into his pocket and pulled out a small blue ghost bead.

Kaz stared. "That's from Mom's necklace!" he exclaimed.

"I know," Little John said. "She was at that house with the other ghost family, but that was before I got there. They told her there were ghosts in the library, too. So she left to find the library. She wanted to see if *we* were the ghosts there."

Kaz reached into his pocket and

pulled out his own ghost bead. It was exactly like Little John's bead.

"You have one, too!" Little John cried. "That means Mom was here. So where'd she go?"

Kaz shook his head. "Mom wasn't ever here," he said. "I think Finn was here for a while before I got here. But Mom was never here."

"Then where did you get that bead?" Little John asked.

"I found it in Claire's school," Kaz replied. "But Mom's not there anymore, either. I don't know where she is."

Little John sighed. "Why can't people

in our family stay in one place? Then maybe we could find them!"

"Claire and I are trying to find everyone," Kaz said. "That's one reason why we started C & K Ghost Detectives."

Little John looked doubtful. "I can't believe that solid girl really wants to help you find our family."

"Solids aren't so bad, Little John," Kaz said. "Most of them are really nice, once you get to know them."

Little John turned to Beckett. "Is that true?" he asked.

Beckett didn't answer right away. But when he did, he said, "No comment."

* * * * * * * * * * * * * * *

"I don't want to meet her," Little John hissed as he, Kaz, and Cosmo hovered in

the kitchen doorway the next morning. "I don't want to meet your solid friend."

It was Saturday, so Claire was still in her pajamas. She sat at the kitchen counter eating her breakfast. She hadn't noticed Kaz and Little John yet. But Claire's cat, Thor, saw the ghosts. He let out an angry yowl as he strolled beneath them.

Cosmo growled at Thor.

Claire turned. "Oh, good morning, Kaz," she said with a smile. She wiped her mouth with her napkin. "Who's your friend?"

Grandma Karen stood in front of the stove flipping pancakes. She turned to see what Claire was talking about.

Little John glowed in fright when he saw Grandma Karen.

"Oh my." Grandma Karen's eyes widened. "I can see *that* ghost."

"That's because he's glowing," Claire said.

Little John backstroked into the living room, away from the kitchen. "You didn't tell me about that other solid!" he cried.

"That's Claire's grandma. Don't worry. She won't hurt us," Kaz said. "And even if she wanted to hurt you, she can't see you if you don't glow, and she can't hear you if you don't wail."

"What's wrong with her hair?" Little John asked. "Why does it have a pink stripe?"

"I don't know." Kaz shrugged. "It just does."

Claire tiptoed into the living room. "Kaz?" she asked.

Little John had stopped glowing, but Claire could still see him.

"Claire, this is my brother Little John.

Little John, this is Claire," Kaz said.

Claire *sloooowly* offered her hand to Little John.

Little John glanced nervously at Kaz. "What's she doing?" he asked. "I can't shake her hand. My hand would pass right through hers."

"I know," Claire spoke directly to Little John. "We can try to shake hands, anyway. Unless you don't like to pass through solid objects, either."

Little John swallowed hard. "Kaz is the scaredy ghost. Not me. *I* can pass through solid objects." He reached for Claire's hand and they shook hands as best they could.

"Scaredy ghost, huh?" Claire asked Kaz.

Kaz made a face.

"That's what our grandpop called

Kaz," Little John said with a slow smile. Claire laughed, and just like that, they were all friends.

Kaz and Claire showed Little John around the library. Then they told Little John about the five o'clock ghost. Claire even showed him her detective notebook, while Beckett looked on.

"We don't have any good clues for solving this case," Claire said. "All we have are observations. The Jeffreys' garage door goes up. A lamp comes on in their living room. A voice comes through all their TVs, and there are wavy lines on the screens. The voice even comes through their organ. And it all happens at five o'clock. It goes on for fifteen or twenty minutes. Then it stops. It could be ghosts doing all that. It could be David's big sister. It could be somebody

else. We have no idea what's going on."

"Sounds like some sort of electromagnetic interference to me," Beckett said.

"What's that?" Claire asked.

"You're in a library," Beckett said. "Look it up."

Claire pulled out her phone. "How do you spell it?"

"Not on your phone," Beckett groaned. "Look it up in a book!"

"Why?" Claire asked. "What's the difference? Never mind. I found an article about it." She squinted as she read. "I don't get what it is."

"Maybe you'd get it if you read about it in a *book*," Beckett said. Then he passed through the bookshelf and went into his secret room.

"This says it has something to do with

radio frequency," Claire said, reading from her phone.

"So, not ghosts?" Kaz said.

Claire shook her head. "It looks like a bunch of things can cause interference. Radio and TV stations, maybe even cell phones."

"Cell phones?" Kaz said. "So maybe Ally *is* doing something with her cell phone."

"Could be," Claire said, tapping her finger against her chin. "Maybe she doesn't know she's doing it. Maybe her phone is causing some sort of interference."

"How can we find out for sure?" Kaz asked.

Claire grinned. "I have an idea. But we're going to need your little brother's help."

CHAPTER 8

A DANGEROUS MISSION

Me?" Little John cried. "How can I help?"

Yeah! Kaz wondered, trying not to feel jealous. *What can Little John do to help?*

"Remember, David's mom said that he and Ben have dentist appointments on Monday," Claire said.

"So?" Kaz said.

"So, Ally's probably going to go hang out with her friends," Claire said.

"Which means no one will be home at David's house. I wonder if the ghost"—Claire made air quotes with her fingers—"will still come out if no one's home."

That's a good question, Kaz thought.

Claire went on, "Little John can pass through walls. So maybe he can go inside David's house on Monday and find out for us."

"That is a terrible idea," Beckett said. "A terribly *dangerous* idea."

"It's not that I can't pass through walls—" Kaz started to say.

"I know," Claire interrupted. She and Little John continued at the same time: "You just don't like to."

"*I* like to pass through walls," Little John said. He spun around and plunged headfirst through the fiction-room wall

and disappeared. "See?" he called from the next room over.

Then he stepped back through the wall. "But how am I going to get inside this boy's house? Won't I have to go into the Outside to get there? The wind will blow me right past it."

Claire held up her water bottle. "This is how Kaz travels outside," she said. "If I can put my water bottle right up against David's house, maybe you can pass through the bottle *and* the house."

"Oh," Little John said. "Okay."

What could possibly go wrong?

* * * * * * * * * * * * * * *

"No!" Beckett said on Monday. "You cannot send that little boy into a house all by himself. It's too dangerous!"

"Mind your own business, Beckett!"

Claire said as she twisted the top from her bottle.

Kaz, Little John, and Cosmo all shrank down . . . down . . . down. Kaz swam into the bottle through the open top, and Little John and Cosmo passed through the stars on the side of the bottle.

The bottle felt crowded with three ghosts. They all had to shrink a little smaller to fit, which made everything in the Outside look even bigger. And scarier.

"I'm telling you, this is a bad idea," Beckett said, following them all the way to the front door. "A really *bad* idea."

"I can do it, Beckett," Little John said. "Don't worry."

Kaz felt proud of his little brother, but also a little bit jealous. *Proud. Jealous. Proud. Jealous.* It was as though those

feelings were playing tug-of-war inside Kaz's heart.

"I'm opening the door now, Beckett," Claire said, putting her hand on the doorknob. "You better get out of the way."

"Hmph," Beckett said as he backstroked away from the door.

Claire walked Kaz, Little John, and Cosmo down the street, the bottle swinging gently at her side.

"This is . . . weird," Little John said after a while.

"What's weird?" Kaz asked.

"We're in the Outside, but not really," Little John said, looking all around.

"We're traveling *safely* in the Outside," Kaz said. "Now let's see if we can solve this case." They were close to solving it; Kaz could feel it.

As they turned onto David's street, Kaz saw the same lady working in her flower garden and listening to music on her radio.

Wait . . . radio? Claire said something about radios when she was reading about the electro-whatever interference.

"Claire?" Kaz called out. "CLAIRE!" Now that he was smaller than usual, he had to talk even louder to get Claire's attention.

"What?" she said, raising the bottle to the level of her eyes.

Kaz pointed at the radio on the grass. "Could that radio over there be causing the interference and making all those strange things happen at David's house?"

Claire turned. "That little thing? I don't know. We have a radio like that at home, and it never causes any problems

with our TV. But . . . if we're right about the interference thing, maybe *she's* having interference, too. Let's go see."

She skipped over. "Hello again," Claire said, stopping right beside the radio.

The lady glanced up. "Oh hello," she said, shading her eyes. "You're that Jeffrey boy's friend, aren't you?"

"Yes," Claire replied. "Did you know that some strange things have been happening over at their house?"

"Strange things?"

"Yeah," Claire said. "Like, their garage door goes up all by itself. And a lamp comes on. They also get these lines on their TVs, and they hear a really weird voice both on their TVs and through their organ."

"Through their organ? Really?" The lady shifted her legs.

"Yeah. And these things always happen at five o'clock. I was just wondering if you have any trouble with your radio at five o'clock?"

"Well, now that you mention it, I do tend to get a little static around five o'clock," the lady admitted. "I don't know why. It's fine any other time."

"Strange," Claire said.

So . . . whatever was happening, it wasn't *only* happening at David's house.

"We should talk to more people on this street," Kaz said when they were on their way again. "Maybe other people are having problems, too."

"Maybe," Claire said. She checked her phone. "We've got a few minutes before five o'clock. We can talk to a couple of neighbors."

She ran over to the next house and

rang the bell. A woman with a crying baby in her arms opened the door. "Yes?" she said in a tired voice as she jiggled the baby.

"I was wondering," Claire began. "Have you noticed anything strange happening in your house at five o'clock? Like, does your garage door go up by itself? Or does a light come on? Or do you get strange lines on your TV screen?"

The woman scowled. "I don't know what you're selling, but I don't have time for it. Sorry." She slammed her door.

Kaz, Cosmo, and Little John all jumped.

"That was mean," Little John said.

Claire tried the next house. Nobody was home.

"We probably have time to try one more, then we should go over to David's house," Claire said as she climbed the steps to the third house. David's house was two houses away.

Kaz noticed light flickering inside the front window. "WAIT!" he yelled just before Claire's finger touched the doorbell.

"What?" she said.

"There's a TV on inside that house," Kaz said.

"So?" Claire said.

"So I think it would be interesting to see if anything strange comes on *this* TV at five o'clock," Kaz said. "We know no one's home at the Jeffreys' house. If something happens at this house at five o'clock, we know it has nothing to do with anyone in David's family, *or*

with any ghosts who might be hiding at David's house."

Claire walked over to the window. "I can't see the TV very well," she said.

"You could send me inside *this* house instead of that other one," Little John suggested. "Then I can tell you if anything happens at five o'clock."

"Well," Claire said. "Okay. But I'm not sure about sending you into this house. Someone might see me on the porch." She skipped back down the stairs, looked around, then darted into the side yard. She crouched down and crept *sloooowly* over to the house and hid behind some bushes.

"Okay, Little John," she said, pressing her water bottle against the house. "I'll keep the bottle right here. Make sure that when you come back, you pass

back through in exactly the same spot you go through now."

"I will," Little John said.

Kaz grabbed Cosmo to make sure the ghost dog didn't follow Little John.

"Wee!" Little John cried. "This will be FUN!" He turned a somersault and passed through the bottle into the house.

Kaz sighed. Did Little John always have to do something fancy when he passed through something?

Then Kaz, Cosmo, and Claire waited. And waited.

And waited some more.

"My arm is getting tired," Claire said as she shifted position and switched

which hand was holding her water bottle.

"You can't let go!" Kaz cried. "You can't move that bottle at all. Not even an inch." If she did, when Little John came back, he could miss the bottle and blow away in the wind.

"I know," Claire said. She glanced up at the sky. "I wonder what time it is. It's starting to get dark."

Still holding the bottle tight against the house, Claire pulled out her phone and checked the display. "It's five forty, Kaz. Your brother should have come out by now."

Uh-oh. *Did something bad happen to Little John? Did he pass through in the wrong place and get lost somewhere else in the Outside?*

There was only one thing to do.

"Cosmo and I have to go in," Kaz said. "We have to find Little John."

"You don't like to pass through solid objects," Claire said.

"I know," Kaz said. But he didn't have a choice. *Don't think about it,* he told himself. *Just do it. Like with the button on the organ. And the sword.*

"Okay, here we go." He grabbed his dog, took a deep breath, then plunged

through the side of the water bottle and into the side of the house.

The wall was thicker than Kaz expected. It pushed back against his body for a second. Holding tight to Cosmo, Kaz kicked his legs as hard as he could. He could feel the wall slicing through him. It made him feel sooooo skizzy. But he just kept kicking until he was all the way through.

Once he and Cosmo were safe, he let go of his dog and shook himself. "I did it!" he said with a short laugh. "I really did it."

"Woof! Woof!" Cosmo barked.

Now to find Little John.

Kaz looked all around. He was in someone's bedroom. A young boy's, he guessed from all the toy trucks.

"Little John?" he called as he swam

out into the hallway. Cosmo swam right beside him. "Where are you, Little John?"

Kaz and Cosmo continued down the hallway and into the living room. A TV was on in the corner, and two solid boys, who looked a little older than Little John but not quite as old as Kaz, stood over a pair of toy cars that appeared to be driving around the floor all by themselves. Each boy held a strange object that had a bunch of buttons and dials. Little John hovered above them.

"There you are!" Kaz cried.

Little John turned. "Kaz!" he exclaimed. "You passed through the wall?"

"Yes," Kaz said. "Because you didn't come back. Why didn't you come back?"

"Because! Look!" Little John pointed at the cars on the floor. "Those are called remote-control cars. Those boys are

making the cars move with those things in their hands."

The solid boys, of course, had no idea that two ghost boys were watching them.

Kaz frowned. He wasn't sure if he felt relieved that Little John was okay or annoyed that Little John was in here having fun while he and Claire were in the Outside worrying.

"You were sent in here to do a job, Little John," Kaz said, hands on his hips. "You were supposed to watch and observe what happened at five o'clock."

"I did," Little John said.

"And?" Kaz said. "Did you see anything?"

"I saw lines on the TV. And there was a weird voice on the TV, too. Just like you heard in that other house," Little John said. "But it's not there anymore."

"Was the voice scary?" Kaz asked.

"Yes," Little John said. "But those boys weren't scared. They were *mad* because they couldn't hear their show."

"Could you understand the voice?" Kaz asked.

"A little," Little John said. "I heard 'W . . . B . . . Zero . . . something.' Then I heard, 'Whiskey, Bravo, Zero, Leema, Bravo, Bravo . . .' and 'Little Boy Blue,' and 'same time tomorrow.'"

So, some of the same words Kaz and Claire had heard at David's house. But there were other words and phrases, too.

"Did you see any ghosts?" Kaz asked.

"Nope."

"Did you see anything else that could have made that voice come out of the TV?" Kaz asked.

"Nope." Little John shook his head.

So who was causing all this mischief in David's neighborhood? And was that person solid or ghost?

* * * * * * * * * * * * * * * *

"Maybe we should forget about the electromagnetic interference idea for now and focus on the words we heard coming through the TVs and David's organ," Claire suggested later that night at the library.

Little John was playing with Cosmo. Beckett was reading a book. And Kaz and Claire were going over everything Claire had written in her notebook.

W . . . B . . . Zero . . .

Whiskey, Bravo, Zero, Leema, Bravo, Bravo.

Little Boy Blue.

Same time tomorrow.

"I don't get it," Claire said.

"Well, 'Little Boy Blue' is a nursery rhyme," Little John offered. "Don't you remember, Kaz? Grandmom used to say it. 'Little Boy Blue, come blow your horn.'"

Kaz remembered. He said the rest of the words with Little John: "The sheep's in the meadow, the cow's in the corn. But where is the boy who looks after the sheep? He's under the haystack, fast asleep."

"Okay," Claire said. "But what does that rhyme have to do with the strange things that are going on in David's neighborhood?"

Kaz and Little John both shrugged.

Claire turned back to her notebook. "Little Boy Blue is going to look after the sheep the same time tomorrow?" she suggested. "Or Little Boy Blue is going to fall asleep the same time tomorrow?"

"At five o'clock?" Kaz said.

"Five o'clock is awfully early to go to bed." Claire leaned back against her chair. "And where does Whiskey, Bravo, Zero, Leema, Bravo, Bravo come in? What does it all mean?"

"If only there were a place, like a library, where you could look something up," Beckett said as he turned the page in his book.

"There is," Claire said. "It's called the Internet!" She leaped from her chair.

Beckett groaned. "Doesn't anyone look things up in books anymore?"

The ghosts followed Claire to the fiction room. The library was closed, so Claire had her choice of computers.

She sat down at the first computer and started typing. "Hmm," she said, squinting at the screen. "I guess it's spelled L–I–M–A, not L–E–E–M–A." She typed

in more of the words they heard, and
something new came up on the screen.

"NATO phonetic alphabet?" Kaz
read over her shoulder. "What is *that*?"

"I don't know," Claire said. She
typed NATO PHONETIC ALPHABET, and
another article came up on the computer.
"It looks like a code or something,"
she said, scrolling through the article.

"When people are talking and it's hard to understand each other, they use the NATO phonetic alphabet to spell the words that are hard to understand. Whiskey, Lima, and Bravo are all part of that alphabet." Claire shook her head. "But W-B-Zero-L-B-B doesn't spell anything."

"Why don't you type W-B-Zero-L-B-B into the computer," Kaz suggested. "Maybe it means something we don't know."

Claire typed in WB0LBB, and everyone watched what came up on the screen:

AMATEUR RADIO LICENSE—WB0LBB— J. C. HILL

"J. C. Hill," Claire said. "That's the name that was on that magazine that was accidentally delivered to David's house!

That's David's neighbor! I wonder if he has something to do with all this."

"Maybe we should go meet him tomorrow after school and find out," Kaz suggested.

"Do I have to go with you?" Little John asked.

"You don't want to come with us?" Kaz replied, surprised.

Little John shrugged. "It sounds boring. I'd rather stay here and play with Cosmo. And Beckett. Will you read me a story, Beckett?"

"I suppose," Beckett said.

So the next day Claire and Kaz went back to David's neighborhood alone. Kaz was sort of glad Little John didn't want to come. He didn't have to worry about his little brother getting distracted. And he didn't have to worry about Cosmo.

Claire remembered exactly which house she'd delivered that magazine to the other day. She marched up the steps to the front porch and rang the bell.

A man with curly white hair opened the door. "Yes? Can I help you?" he asked.

"Is your name J. C. Hill?" Claire asked.

"Yes," the man said warily. "And you are?"

"Claire. Claire Kendall. Do you have an amateur radio license?"

"Why, yes I do." J. C. looked pleasantly surprised. "Why do you ask? I didn't think kids today were all that interested in amateur radio."

"Well, I don't know much about it," Claire admitted. "But I was wondering, could an amateur radio make a garage door go up all by itself? Could it make a

lamp turn on without pressing the switch? And could it make wavy lines come up on TV screens, and scary voices come through TVs and organs?"

J. C. groaned. "Are you a neighbor? Are you having some interference?" He stepped out onto his porch.

"I'm not your neighbor, so I'm not having any problems," Claire said. "I'm a detective! I'm trying to figure out why your neighbors are having problems." She told him what was happening at some of the other houses in the neighborhood.

J. C. groaned again. "I'm sorry," he said. "I don't know the neighbors. This is my daughter's house. I've had some recent health problems, so I moved in with her a couple of weeks ago. My son-in-law just got my radio set up last weekend so I could talk to my radio group in Florida. I check in with my buddies every day at five o'clock our time. I had no idea the neighbors were having trouble."

"We don't know for sure that your radio is causing the trouble," Claire said. "We just think it might be."

"Well, let's find out if it is," J. C. said.

Claire took J. C. to meet the neighbors. Kaz listened from inside Claire's bottle. Several of the closest neighbors said they'd noticed some wavy lines and strange voices coming through their TVs around five o'clock. But the two houses on either side of J. C.'s house seemed to have the most trouble.

"I'm sorry if my radio is causing interference," J. C. said to Mrs. Jeffrey, David, and Ben as they stood on the

Jeffreys' front porch. "Would you mind turning on your television right now? I'd like to see whether my radio is causing your trouble."

"Sure," Mrs. Jeffrey said. "I'd like to know, too. Whatever's causing it, I was pretty sure it wasn't a ghost." She ruffled Ben's hair.

"Ghost?" J. C. chuckled. "Did you think I was a ghost, little man?"

Ben shrugged and hid behind his mom.

J. C. grinned. "If my radio is causing interference, I have some ideas for fixing it," he told Mrs. Jeffrey. Then he turned to Claire. "Would you like to see what amateur radio is all about?"

"Sure," Claire said, hugging her bottle to her hip.

"Can I see, too?" David asked.

"Me too!" Ben begged.

"Why don't you stay here with me, Ben, and we'll see if we get interference on our TV," Mrs. Jeffrey said.

Ben groaned. But then his face brightened. "Can we see if the voice comes through the organ again?"

"Yes, we'll turn on both the organ and the TV and see what happens,"

Mrs. Jeffrey said, leading Ben back inside the house.

Claire and David walked next door with J. C. Once inside, J. C. led them to a small room off the kitchen.

"Welcome to my shack," he said, waving his hand around the room. It had one large table with a bunch of electronics stuff. There wasn't much else. A small window looked out into the backyard.

"Why do you call it a shack?" David asked.

J. C. grinned. "That's what we hams call our radio setup," he said as he sat down heavily on the stool.

"Hams?" Claire scrunched up her nose.

"That's another word for amateur radio operators," he said.

J. C. turned on one of the machines,

and Claire and Ben stood on either side of him.

That machine was way bigger than any other radio Kaz had ever seen. And there was no music, just talking. Sometimes the talking was hard to understand, especially when J. C. turned the big dial. One voice faded and another came on. He turned the dial a little farther and then stopped.

The radio was silent.

"It's not five o'clock yet, but let's see if any of my friends are listening," J. C. said as he reached for a microphone. "K-A-0-I-A-O . . . K-A-0-I-A-O . . . K-A-0-I-A-O, this is W-B-0-L-B-B calling. Little Boy Blue calling K-A-0-I-A-O."

"What's Little Boy Blue?" Claire asked.

"That's me." J. C. grinned. "I'm Little Boy Blue. *B*s are hard to understand on the

radio. A *B* sounds like *D*, *E*, *G*, *P,* *T*, or *V*. Sometimes I say Lima, Bravo, Bravo, but Little Boy Blue sounds more interesting, doesn't it?"

Claire and David agreed that it did.

J. C. turned back to his microphone. "K-A-0-I-A-O . . . K-A-0-I-A-O . . . This is W-B-0-L-B-B. Are you around, Donna?"

A couple of seconds later, a scratchy

lady's voice came over the radio. "W-B-0-L-B-B. This is K-A-0-I-A-O. Wasn't expecting to hear from you until dinnertime."

"Let's go see if J. C. is on our TV or our organ right now," David said.

"Okay. Keep talking, Mr. Hill," Claire said as she held tight to her water bottle. "We'll be right back."

She and David ran next door. David's garage door stood open, so they went into the house through the garage.

"It's coming through the TV and the organ again. And it's not even five o'clock!" Ben exclaimed as soon as David and Claire walked into the living room.

Kaz noticed that the table lamp was on, too.

They saw the lines on the TV, and they heard J. C.'s garbled voice coming through both the TV and the organ. Now that they'd actually met J. C., they recognized the voice as his. It didn't sound nearly as scary anymore. In fact, it sounded kind of funny.

Claire and David returned to J. C.'s house as he was finishing his conversation with K-A-0-I-A-O.

J. C. spun on his stool to face the kids.

"Did you notice any interference?" he asked.

"Yes. The garage door was up, the lamp was on, and your voice came through the TV and the organ again," David said.

"I'm sorry to hear that," J. C. said. "But I'm pretty sure we can fix all of it. At your house and anyone else's. We'll get a couple of filters, maybe wrap some wire. I'll see if my son-in-law can help with that this weekend."

"Okay," David said. "I'll tell my mom. It was nice to meet you."

"Nice to meet you, too," J. C. said.

* * * * * * * * * * * * * * *

Claire's parents returned from their convention later that evening.

"So, what have you been up to while

we've been away?" Claire's dad asked as he gave her a hug.

"Not much," Claire said.

"What do you mean 'not much'?" Kaz said. "We solved another case!"

"I met an amateur radio operator," Claire said.

"That sounds interesting," Claire's dad said.

While Claire was talking to her parents, Kaz went to join Little John, Beckett, and Cosmo in the craft room.

"Ready to practice some ghost skills, Kaz?" Beckett asked.

"Did you know Kaz can pass through walls now?" Little John asked Beckett.

"You can?" Beckett asked.

"I could always pass through walls," Kaz grumbled.

"So you've said." Beckett folded his

arms across his chest. "But I've never seen you do it."

"Fine. I'll show you!" Kaz swam over to the wall. The one that didn't have any bookshelves or cabinets. It should be easier to pass through a wall like that than it was to pass through both Claire's water bottle and the side of David's house.

Don't think about it. Just do it, Kaz told himself. He took a deep breath, closed his eyes, plugged his nose, and slid through the wall into the entryway. Once he was through, he opened his eyes and shook himself. *That wasn't so bad!*

He turned and passed back through to the craft room. "See?" he said to Beckett.

"Well, it's about time," Beckett said. "Maybe now you'll come visit my secret room."

"Secret room?" Little John's eyes lit up. "What secret room?"

"It's behind that bookcase over there." Beckett pointed.

Little John didn't wait for an invitation. He charged right through the wall of books.

A few seconds later, Little John called out from the other side of the wall. "Kaz! You've got to see this!"

BY EDGAR AWARD WINNER **DORI HILLESTAD BUTLER**

The HAUNTED LIBRARY

THE SECRET ROOM